Darwin

Mooch

Juarez

STARRING

Speckles

Blaster

Bucky

Hurley

First published by Parragon in 2009
Parragon
Queen Street House
4 Queen Street
Bath BA1 1HE, UK

ISBN 978-1-4075-6061-8

Printed in China

Parragon

Bath · New York · Singapore · Hong Kong · Cologne · Delhi · Melbourne

Agent Darwin is no ordinary guinea pig… he is the leader of a specially trained **top-secret** government unit called the G-Force.

Fellow guinea pigs, **Juarez** and **Blaster**, along with a fly named **Mooch** and a mole named **Speckles**, complete **Darwin's** team.

The G-Force have been training for their first big mission and, finally, the assignment they have all been waiting for has come in.

Ben Kendall, the man behind G-Force tells them they are to infiltrate the home of Leonard Saber.

There is intelligence that Saber is planning something called **Project Clusterstorm**. It looks like Saber is going to use his Saberling 5000 appliances to take over the world!

TOP SECRET

MISSION: To uncover the truth about Leonard Saber's Clusterstorm project.

ACTION: Sneak into Saber's mansion, hack into his computer and download Project Clusterstorm files.

Later, with **Speckles** feeding intelligence to the team, the G-Force agents successfully enter the Saber mansion undetected.

Once inside, Agent Darwin makes his way to Saber's study, plugs his PDA into Saber's computer and downloads the **top-secret** Clusterstorm files.

Mission accomplished

or is it?

Go Team!

Back at the bio lab inside an old warehouse, Ben and the team await the arrival of the **FBI agents** who are going to evaluate the G-Force. The team is eager to show them what they have recovered at Saber's.

Then disaster strikes! The files are corrupt and Speckles can't run the computer properly. They have wasted the FBI's time!

"This entire lab is an embarrassment," FBI agent Kip Killian tells Ben.

"I'm shutting you down!"

And it gets worse! Killian wants to take the G-Force into custody!

There's no time to lose.

 The animals quickly jump into escape pods and shoot out of their headquarters and into the outside world. They land on the loading dock behind the lab where a young man is unloading supplies. Darwin looks around and spots an empty pet carrier. He orders the team inside and shuts the door behind them.

 Moments later, the carrier is picked up and put in a truck which heads away from the warehouse. They are safe – **for now.**

When the truck finally stops, Darwin and his team find themselves in a whole new world – a cage inside Elia's Pet Shop.

"Guys, we need to find a way out of here," Darwin says, scanning the inside of their cage for an exit.

"Don't move!" a voice suddenly shouts. Turning around, the team find a vicious hamster staring at them, his paws raised in warning.

"Take it easy buddy," Darwin says calmly.

"For your information, it's Bucky!" shouts the hamster.

Bucky is interrupted by the sound of a fart so loud, it blows wood chips everywhere!

It's Hurley. A roly-poly guinea pig who is more than happy to laze around all day.

"Locate escape options," Darwin instructs his team. **They need to get away – fast!**

PARP!

If Darwin had only known what would happen…

All too soon, Juarez and Blaster are bought by two children who have some interesting plans for their new pets.

Now it is just agents Darwin and Speckles in the cage with Bucky and Hurley. The remaining G-Force members come up with a plan. Speckles will play dead in the hope that the pet shop owners will bury him in the garden.

"Once I'm in the ground, I can tunnel to freedom and rescue you," he promises Darwin.

But Speckles' plan backfires. When Terrell, the pet shop employee, sees the dead mole, he takes the body and throws it in the back of a trash truck!

Darwin is devastated. Will Speckles have survived?

More determined than ever to escape, Darwin manages to find a way out of the pet store. But once again, he runs into trouble – in the form of Hurley. The big guinea pig ends up tagging along, which isn't exactly what Darwin had planned.

With no choice, Darwin begins to lead Hurley back towards Ben's house. Along the way, they pass an electrical appliance store. A Saberling coffee maker is on display in the window.

"Hurley, I gotta check out that coffee maker," says Darwin. "Stay close."

Suddenly the coffee maker comes
to life and tries to attack Darwin!
He bravely fights the machine and
manages to disable it.

Darwin pulls out the microchip inside the
coffee machine.

"Do you know what this is?" he asks Hurley.
"It's military grade. Developed for the Unmanned
Weapons Programme. I've got to get this chip back
to Ben!"

Darwin and Hurley burst in to Ben's house and finds him eating pizza with Juarez and Blaster. The other G-Force agents had escaped from the home of the two children that had bought them from the pet shop.

Darwin fills them in on Speckles' sad death and the truth about Saber's coffee machine. Then he tells them the worst part – the programme is set to go off in thirty minutes! There is no time to lose!

Ben, Juarez and Blaster are horrified.

Ben decides it's time to reveal G-Force's new weapon, the RDV.

"It's a little prototype I've been working on, called the Rapid Deployment Vehicle. She'll do 65 with the throttle wide open," he explains.

"Everybody in the RDV!" shouts Darwin. "Juarez, plot a course to Saber's!"

TOP SECRET

The G-Force arrive at Saber's mansion – but they're too late! **Project Clusterstorm has already been activated!**

Across the world, Saberling appliances start coming to life…

Things get worse – the individual machines are joining forces and then magnets begin to suck space junk from the skies – **the Earth is in chaos!**

Crash! Smash!

Darwin heads deeper into the Saber mansion. He has a new plan. He'll find the computer that controls **Clusterstorm** and disable it with a virus.

As Darwin enters the inner complex of Saber computers, he sees something he didn't expect to see – Speckles! His face breaks out into a huge smile. Speckles is alive!

But Darwin's joy is short lived. It turns out that Speckles was the mastermind behind **Project Clusterstorm** all along!

"How could you do this to us?" Darwin asks in disbelief. "I thought we were friends. I put my life on the line for you."

Speckles laughs. Friends? Maybe, but Speckles explains to Darwin that he couldn't let friendship get in the way. Speckles has never forgiven mankind for killing his entire family. Clusterstorm is his revenge. As he speaks, Speckles presses a button. Suddenly, the appliances come together to form a giant metal beast.

Darwin realizes it's too late to save Speckles, but it's not too late to save Earth! The brave guinea pig heads into battle, his team close behind.

But it's an uneven battle – the Clusterstorm beast is getting **larger and larger** with every machine that joins onto it. There's no way of defeating such a monster…

Just when it looks like all hope is lost, Darwin manages to insert the computer virus into the beast's control system.

The giant beast begins to fall apart and crashes to the ground, smashing into hundreds of pieces as it lands.

"No! No! No!" screams Speckles as his plan falls apart.

"NoOOOOO!"

The threat of project Clusterstorm has been removed and Earth is safe – all thanks to the G-Force.

The gang are rewarded for their hard work and the unit is finally reinstated by the FBI – they're once again legitimate agents. And they even get some new members – Hurley and Bucky!

"G-Force!"

shout the gang in unison, as they
thrust their fists into the air!
They can't wait for their next mission.

The End